VIRTUE STORIES

I am not Scared

Lalita Iyer

Om KIDZ

An imprint of Om Books International

Maya got a big fat zero in the Maths test. Again. She had forgotten to tell Mama about it on Friday; and now Mama had to sign the paper or they would call Mama tomorrow and complain, which in her experience was far worse.

She was so scared! Mama would be angry. She toyed with trying to copy Mama's signature. She had her homework diary.

She must try. How hard could it be? But when she opened it, her heart sank.

The signature was a swirly-curvy set of dancing letters that she could never copy!

She decided to fall sick instead. Maybe they would forget to ask about the paper the day after!

She thought deeply on the bus back about how to fall sick. To her friend's surprise, she turned down a game of who-can-slap-my-hand-the-quickest (at which she was the undisputed champion). At last, she came up with a plan!

She would have a cold water shower. That would bring on a fever immediately. The only thing was that she hated getting wet in cold water. She decided she would just have to do it, as she was scared about what Mama would do if she found out!

As a backup plan, she decided to tuck two onions into her armpits prior to her bath, and hang out in the bathroom for a bit - she'd read it also induced immediate fever. She hated onions and the smell made her want to barf. She would just have to do it as she was scared of the consequences otherwise.

Later that evening, as Mama made dinner, Maya sat shivering in the bathroom. The onions, skin and all - were safely, but very uncomfortably, sitting under her armpits.

Within a few minutes though, her arms and shoulders ached, her armpits began to scratch. She hid the onions in the drawer full of lotions, perfumes and other toiletries and decided to take a longer-than-planned-for-shower.

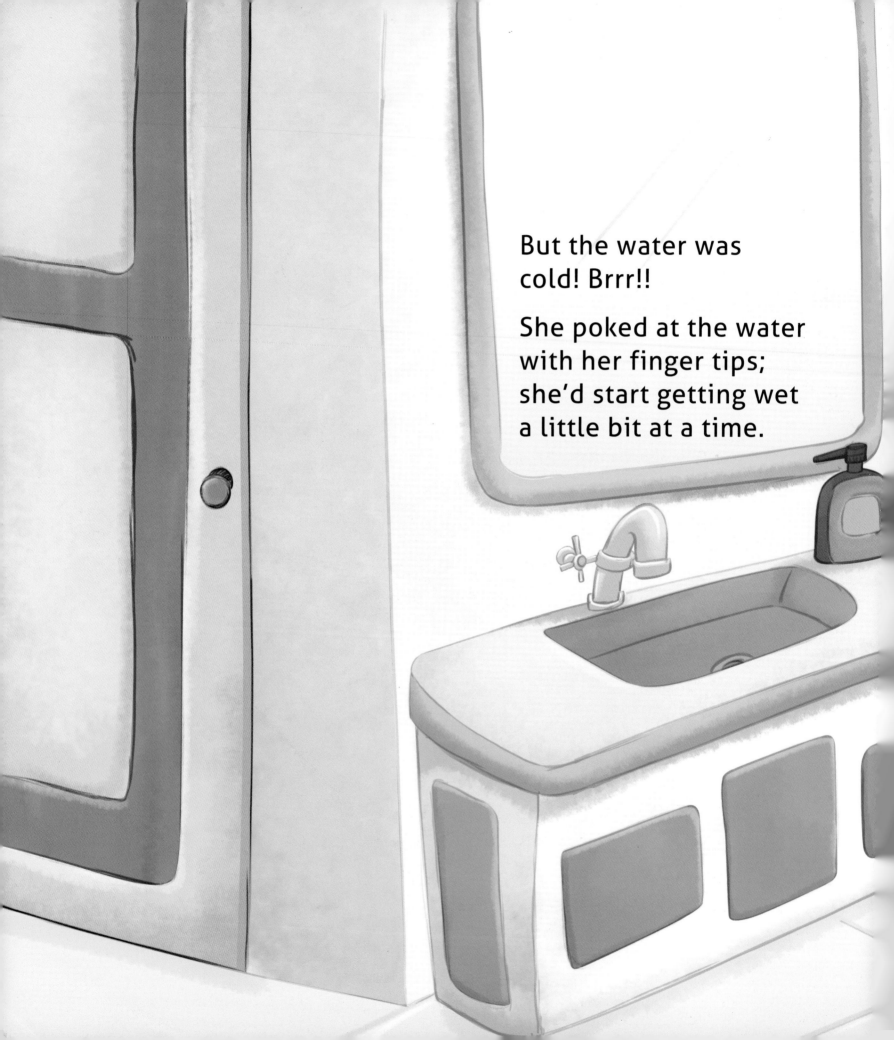

But the water was cold! Brrr!!

She poked at the water with her finger tips; she'd start getting wet a little bit at a time.

Then she stuck out her toes and withdrew them almost instantly. She tried her arms next; dancing sideways and backwards as the icy droplets fell in merry abandon. This wasn't working either.

Maya dried herself and came out. Mama had called her for dinner at least thrice by now. She was very quiet at dinner. Mama asked her if she was fine and she forgot and said 'yes,' and then it was too late to go back and say 'no,' as Nikki began crying and Mama hurried off to give him his bottle.

' Is everything fine, Maya?' Mama asked her as she tucked her into bed. Maya nodded, but the tears began to roll down her cheeks. 'What is the matter Maya?' Mama asked. Maya plucked up courage and decided, *I will not be chicken. I will just do it.* And she told Mama everything.

To her surprise Mama praised her for telling the truth and promised to sign the paper. Maya agreed to wake up early to redo the sums she'd made mistakes on. This feeling of being free was wonderful! Mama was not angry and Maya was not scared any more!